RAINBOW magic ®

The Jewel Fairies

For Danni who loves fairies

Special thanks to
Narinder Dhami

ORCHARD BOOKS
96 Leonard Street, London EC2A 4XD
Hachette Children's Books
Level 17/207 Kent Street,
Sydney, NSW 2000
A Paperback Original
First published in Great Britain in 2005 as 1 84362 958 5
Rainbow Magic is a registered trademark of Working Partners Limited.
Series created by Working Partners Limited, London W6 OQT
Text © Working Partners Limited 2005
Illustrations © Georgie Ripper 2005
The right of Georgie Ripper to be identified as the illustrator
of this work has been asserted by her in accordance
with the Copyright, Designs and Patents Act, 1988.
A CIP catalogue record for this book is available
from the British Library.
ISBN 1 84616 099 5
3 5 7 9 10 8 6 4 2
Printed in Great Britain

India
the Moonstone
Fairy

by Daisy Meadows

illustrated by Georgie Ripper

ORCHARD BOOKS

www.rainbowmagic.co.uk

The Fairyland Palace

Adventure Playground

Tippington Manor

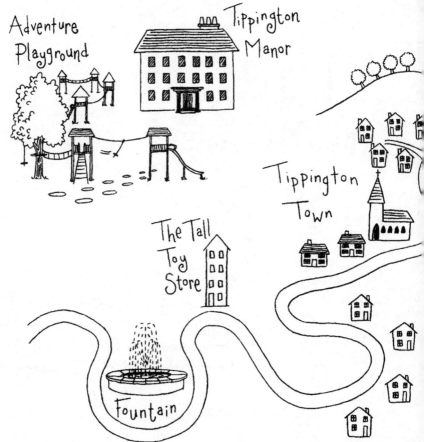

Tippington Town

The Tall Toy Store

Fountain

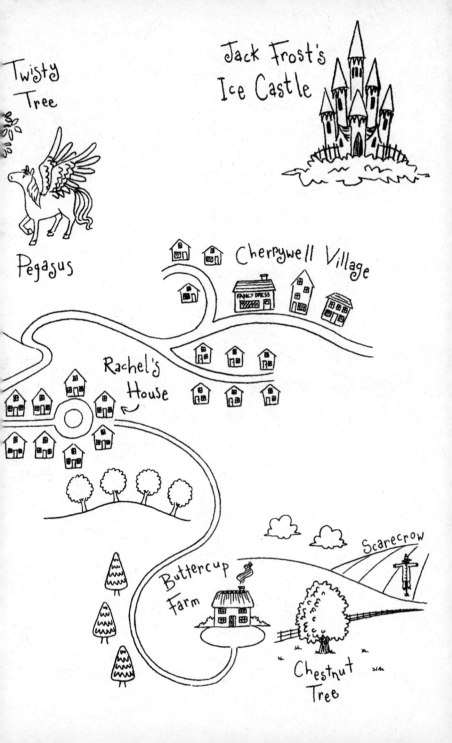

By Frosty magic I cast away
These seven jewels with their fiery rays,
So their magic powers will not be felt
And my icy castle shall not melt.

The fairies may search high and low
To find the gems and take them home.
But I will send my goblin guards
To make the fairies' mission hard.

Contents

A Nasty Nightmare

"Kirsty, help!" Rachel Walker shouted.
"The goblins are going to get me!"

Panting, Rachel glanced behind her.
She was running as fast as she could,
but the green goblins were getting closer
and closer. They were grinning nastily,
showing their pointed teeth. Now one
of them had grabbed Rachel by the

shoulder, and was shaking her hard—

"Rachel?" Kirsty Tate was leaning over her friend's bed, shaking her awake. "Wake up! You're having a nightmare."

Rachel woke and sat up in bed. "What time is it?" she asked. "I dreamt that there were horrible goblins chasing me, and I couldn't escape."

"It's 7.30," Kirsty replied, perching on the edge of the bed. "Why were the goblins after you?"

Rachel frowned. "I can't remember," she sighed. "But you know what, Kirsty? I've got a funny feeling that Jack Frost might be up to something again!"

Kirsty's eyes opened wide. "Oh, do you really think so?" she gasped. "Then maybe our fairy friends will need our help!"

Rachel and Kirsty shared a magical secret. They had become friends with the fairies, and whenever there was a problem in Fairyland, Kirsty and Rachel were called on to help.

The fairies' greatest enemy was Jack
Frost. He was always looking for ways to
make trouble, helped by his mean goblin
servants. Not long ago, Jack Frost had
tried to ruin the celebration party for
King Oberon and Queen Titania's 1000th
jubilee. But luckily, Kirsty and Rachel
had come to the rescue.

"We'll have to keep our eyes open,"
Rachel agreed. "If the fairies need our
help, they'll let us know somehow."

Kirsty nodded. "Well, it's only the
beginning of half-term, and I'm staying
with you for the whole week," she pointed
out. "So we have plenty of time."

Before Rachel could reply, the sweet,
tinkling sound of music suddenly filled
the room. Both Kirsty and Rachel jumped.

"What's that?" Kirsty asked.

Rachel looked puzzled for a moment,
but then she began to laugh. "It's my
music box!" she smiled, pointing at the
dressing-table. "The one the Party
Fairies gave us."

After helping the Party Fairies to
stop Jack Frost from spoiling the
jubilee celebrations, Rachel and Kirsty
had each been given a beautiful,
musical jewellery box with a tiny
fairy on top. Rachel's box sat on her
dressing-table, and the girls could see
that the fairy was spinning round in
time to the music.

"Yes, but how did
it start up on its
own?" Kirsty
asked, with a
frown. "I didn't
wind it, and
you've only just
woken up."

"Look!" Rachel
gasped. "The box is glowing!"

Rachel scrambled out of bed, and she and Kirsty rushed over to take a closer look. Rachel was right. The box was glowing with a faint pink light which shone from under the closed lid.

"Lift the lid, Rachel," Kirsty whispered.

Hardly daring to breathe, Rachel reached out and slowly lifted the lid.

Immediately a glittering shower of multi-coloured fairy dust burst from the jewellery box. It swirled around the girls, wrapping them in a cloud of sparkles and lifting them off their feet.

Fairy News

After just a moment or two, the sparkles began to drift away and the girls felt their feet lightly touch the ground. Rachel and Kirsty blinked a few times and looked around.

"Kirsty, we're in Fairyland!" Rachel gasped.

"In our pyjamas!" Kirsty added.

The girls were now fairy-sized with glittering fairy wings on their backs, and they were standing in the golden Great Hall of the fairy palace. King Oberon, Queen Titania and a small crowd of fairies stood in front of them. The girls noticed that they all looked worried.

Queen Titania stepped forwards. "You are very welcome, girls," she said with a smile. "I hope you don't mind us bringing you here so unexpectedly."

"Of course not," Rachel said quickly.

"You have been such good friends to us in the past," the Queen went on, "that we were hoping we could call on you again, now that we are in trouble."

"What's wrong?" asked Kirsty anxiously.

"Let me explain," the Queen replied sadly. "Every year, at Halloween, we have a huge celebration in Fairyland. All the fairies have to recharge their fairy magic for another year."

"So every fairy in Fairyland parades around the Grand Square," King Oberon put in. "Then they all march into the palace to a very special chamber, where Queen Titania's tiara rests upon a velvet cushion."

"It sounds wonderful," Rachel sighed, hoping that she and Kirsty might be allowed to watch the grand procession one day.

Queen Titania nodded. "It is," she replied. "And my tiara is very important for fairy magic. It has seven beautiful jewels set in it. A sparkling fountain of fairy dust pours from each of the seven jewels, and they join together to form one great, glittering rainbow of magical fairy dust."

Kirsty and Rachel were listening carefully, their eyes wide.

"What happens then?" Kirsty asked.

"Each fairy must dip her wand in the rainbow fountain to recharge it," the Queen explained. "Then she will be able to perform magic for another year."

The King shook his head sadly. "But now Jack Frost has put a stop to all that," he sighed. "Two nights ago, he crept into the palace and stole the seven jewels from the Queen's tiara!"

"Oh, no!" Rachel and Kirsty exclaimed together.

"Our special celebration was to take place in a week's time," the Queen went on, looking worried. "So the fairies' magic is already running low."

"The jewels must be returned to the tiara," King Oberon added, "before the fairies run out of the jewels' magic completely!"

"Does this mean that there will be no

magic at all left in Fairyland?" asked Kirsty anxiously. "Not exactly," the Queen replied. "Fairy magic isn't quite as simple as that. Some magic, like Weather Magic and Rainbow Magic, aren't controlled by by the jewels."

"But the jewels do control some of the most important kinds of fairy magic," the King explained. "Like flying, wishes and sweet dreams. Some people have already started to have nightmares."

Rachel nodded, thinking of her own scary dream. "We have to get the jewels back!" she said firmly.

"Where is Jack Frost now?" Kirsty wanted to know. "Has he taken the jewels to his ice castle?"

The Queen shook her head. "Jack Frost doesn't have the jewels any more," she said. "Come with me, and I will show you what happened."

Rachel and Kirsty followed the
fairies outside into the beautiful
palace gardens. They
stopped beside the
golden pool, its
surface as clear and
smooth as glass.

"Look," Queen
Titania said
softly, waving
her wand over
the water.

Immediately
tiny ripples began
to spread across the
surface of the pool.
The ripples grew bigger and
bigger, and slowly a picture
appeared on the water's surface.

"It's Jack Frost!" Rachel exclaimed.
Tall, thin, spiky Jack Frost stood
in front of Queen Titania's
golden tiara upon its
velvet cushion. The
seven magic jewels
glittered as dazzling
streams of magic
dust poured
from each one.
Laughing, Jack
Frost thrust his
snowflake-tipped
wand into the
magic rainbow
fountain, where it
glowed like fire.
"He is recharging his
magic," the King explained.

Kirsty and Rachel watched in dismay as Jack Frost then prised the sparkling gems from the golden tiara. He waved his wand and immediately the jewels were encased in solid ice.

"What is he doing?" Rachel asked, puzzled.

"The light and heat of the jewels' magic makes them difficult for cold, icy creatures like Jack Frost and his goblins to hold," Queen Titania explained. "Look."

Now Jack Frost was whizzing back to his ice castle, carried by a frosty wind which blew him along. He carried the jewels in his arms, but Rachel and Kirsty could see that the hard shell of frost around them was already beginning to melt.

Jack Frost swooped down from the grey sky and landed in the throne room of his ice castle. By this time the frost around the jewels had almost melted away. The jewels glowed, casting shimmering rays of light like laser beams into every corner of the icy room. Goblins came running to see the gems, wearing sunglasses to protect their eyes from the glare.

"Stand back, you fools!" Jack Frost roared, waving his wand again and

casting another spell to cover the jewels with ice. But the jewels were still glowing, and the ice began to melt away almost immediately.

"Look, master," yelled one of the goblins suddenly, "the fairy magic is melting your castle!"

Jack Frost looked round in a fury. Sure enough, water was beginning to trickle down the icy walls, and there was a puddle at the foot of his throne.

"Jack Frost's magic is not strong enough to block the power of the jewels," Queen Titania told Rachel and Kirsty.

The girls watched as the goblins began rushing around, mopping up the water as fast as they could. But as quickly as they cleared one puddle away, two more appeared.

"Very well then," shouted Jack Frost, stamping his feet in rage. "If I cannot keep these magic jewels, no one else shall have them! I will cast a spell to get rid of them." And he raised his wand high above his head.

Lost!

"Oh, no!" Kirsty gasped. She and Rachel watched in horror as an icy blast of wind whipped up around the throne room. The glowing jewels were sent spinning and tumbling across the room and out of the window, where they scattered far and wide.

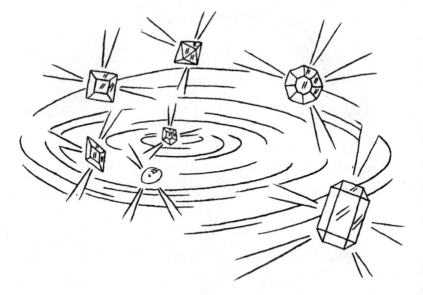

"See how the jewels grow larger as they fall into the human world?" Queen Titania pointed out, just as the picture in the pool began to flicker and fade. "Because they are magical, they'll hide themselves until we can find them and bring them back to Fairyland."

The picture in the pool was fading fast. But just before it disappeared,

Rachel saw one of the jewels,
a creamy-coloured stone,
fall into someone's
back garden. With
a start of surprise,
Rachel realised that
she knew exactly
whose garden it was!

The Queen was shaking
her head sadly as the picture vanished
completely. "All of our fairy seeing
magic is used up," she sighed. "So the
pool can't show us where all the jewels
have gone."

"But I know where one of them is!"
Rachel burst out excitedly. "I recognised
the garden where it fell!"

Everyone turned to stare at her.

"Are you sure, Rachel?" Kirsty asked.

Rachel nodded. "It was Mr and Mrs Palmer's back garden," she explained. "The Palmers are friends of my parents, and I've been to their house loads of times to help Mum babysit their little girl, Ellie."

One of the fairies was so excited at this that she whirled up into the air, her long brown hair streaming out behind her. "I'm India, the Moonstone Fairy," she cried, her eyes shining. "And I'm sure it was my Moonstone which fell into your friends' back garden!"

The little fairy wore a pretty dress with a nipped-in waist and floaty skirt.

The dress was white, but every time India moved, flashes of shimmering pink and blue shot through the material. On her feet she wore dainty white sandals.

"You must meet all our Jewel Fairies," said King Oberon, as the other fairies crowded around. "Each one is responsible for teaching all the other fairies how to use her jewel's magic." He pointed at India the Moonstone Fairy. "India teaches dream magic, while Emily the Emerald Fairy teaches seeing magic, Scarlett the Garnet Fairy teaches growing and shrinking magic, Chloe the Topaz Fairy teaches changing magic, Sophie the Sapphire Fairy teaches wishing magic, Amy the Amethyst Fairy teaches appearing and disappearing magic, and Lucy the Diamond Fairy teaches flying magic."

Rachel and Kirsty smiled round at all the fairies.

"We'll do our best to get your jewels back," Kirsty said.

"Thank you," the fairies replied.

"We knew you would help us," Queen Titania said gratefully. "But Jack Frost knows we will be trying to find the jewels, and he has sent his goblins into the human world to guard them."

"The goblins will find it difficult to pick the jewels up," King Oberon went on. "The bright light and magic of the gems will burn them, because they belong to the cold, icy world of Jack Frost. Instead, the goblins will probably lurk near the jewels and try to stop us getting them back."

Rachel and Kirsty nodded thoughtfully.

Queen Titania looked grave. "So now we need your help not only to find each magic jewel," she finished, "but also to outwit the goblins that will be guarding them!"

On the Right Track

"We'll find a way to get the jewels back," Rachel said firmly, and Kirsty nodded.

King Oberon smiled at them. "And you will have our Jewel Fairies to help you."

Rachel frowned. "I had a dream about the goblins chasing me," she said slowly.

India sighed, looking very sad. "Without the Moonstone, the fairies' power to send sweet dreams into the human world is fading," she explained. "That's why you had a nightmare, Rachel."

"India will return with you to your world," said Queen Titania. "She'll help you find the Moonstone."

"We know we have to look in the Palmers' back garden," Kirsty said. "But how will we know where to search for the other jewels?"

Queen Titania smiled. "Just as before, you must let the magic come to you," she replied. "The jewels will find you.

And remember, they have grown bigger
in the human world, so they will be
easier to spot."

Rachel and Kirsty nodded. Then India
fluttered over to join them and the
Fairy Queen raised her wand.

"Good luck!" called the fairies, as the
Queen waved her wand and Rachel,
Kirsty and India disappeared in a
shower of magic sparkles.

When the cloud of fairy dust vanished, Rachel and Kirsty realised that they were back in Rachel's bedroom.

"We must get to work right away, girls!" called a silvery voice.

The girls turned and saw India perched on the dressing-table mirror.

"Yes, let's go over to the Palmers' house now," said Rachel eagerly, making for the door.

Kirsty burst out laughing. "I think we'd better change out of our pyjamas first, don't you?"

"Good idea!" Rachel grinned.

"How can we get into the Palmers' back garden?" India asked, as the girls quickly got dressed.

"We could throw a ball over the fence," Kirsty suggested. "Then we could ask the Palmers if we can pop into their garden to find it."

"Yes, that would work," Rachel agreed.

"Girls, are you awake?" Mrs Walker's voice drifted up the stairs. "Breakfast's ready."

India fluttered across the room and hid

herself in Kirsty's pocket, and the girls hurried downstairs. "Mum," said Rachel, as she and Kirsty ate toast and jam, "is it OK if we go out to play after breakfast?"

"Yes," Mrs Walker agreed, "but don't go further than the park, and be back in time for lunch."

"Thanks, Mum." Rachel said, slipping out of her chair.

Kirsty did the same. "We need a ball," she whispered as they went to get their jackets.

"There's one in the shed, I think," Rachel replied.

The girls found a tennis ball and then set off down the road. Although it was autumn, it was quite a warm day and the sun shone down brightly from a blue sky.

"I hope my Moonstone is safe," India said softly, popping her head out of Kirsty's pocket. "I wonder if there are any goblins guarding it."

"We'll soon find out," Rachel replied, stopping in front of a house with a bright red door. "This is the Palmers' house."

The house was only three doors away from Rachel's home, on the corner of the street. Rachel took the ball out of her pocket, slipped round the corner and tossed it over the fence into the back garden. Then she joined Kirsty and India again in front of the house.

"I'll knock on the door," Rachel said, leading the way up the path.

"Let's hope they're in!" replied Kirsty.

Rachel rang the bell, and they waited for quite a while. Just as the girls and India were starting to give up hope, the door opened.

"Hello, Rachel," beamed Mrs Palmer. "And you must be Kirsty. Rachel told me she was having a friend to stay."

"Hello," Kirsty said politely.

"Sorry to disturb you, Mrs Palmer," Rachel said, "but I'm afraid we just lost our ball over your fence."

49

Mrs Palmer smiled. "As a matter of fact, I was just sitting in the back garden with Ellie. I didn't see your ball come over, though. Do you want to come and look for it?"

"Yes, please," Rachel replied.

"If you don't mind," added Kirsty.

Mrs Palmer opened the door wide. "Go straight through, girls. I'm just

popping upstairs for a minute. Ellie's in her pram on the patio, if you want to say hello." Rachel led Kirsty through the kitchen and out through the back door.

India popped her head out of Kirsty's pocket. "The Moonstone's here somewhere," she cried happily. "I can feel it!"

"It's a big garden," Kirsty said.

"We better start looking right away." She and India hurried over to the nearest flowerbed and began to peer among the shrubs. Meanwhile, Rachel went across the patio to say hello to Ellie. But as she walked towards the pram with its pretty white sunshade, Rachel began to shiver.

Suddenly there was a chill in the air.
A loud wail came from the pram.

Ellie had started to cry.
Ellie must be feeling
the cold, too, Rachel
thought. But it was
quite warm until
a moment ago!
Mrs Palmer rushed
out of the house and
ran over to the pram. "It's very
strange, Rachel," she said, as she
pushed back the sunshade and bent
down to pick up the baby. "Ellie's
always had trouble sleeping, but ever
since we got this mobile for her pram
yesterday, she's been sleeping ever so
well." Mrs Palmer frowned, lifting
Ellie out from under her lacy blanket.

"Something seems to be upsetting her today though; she's been very restless."

As Mrs Palmer picked Ellie up, the baby stretched out her chubby little hand to grab one of the decorations hanging from the mobile. Rachel looked at it more closely. It was hung with silver stars, yellow suns and pale moons. And then, suddenly, her heart missed a beat, for there, glittering in the middle of the mobile, was a cream-coloured stone which flashed with pink and blue light.

The Moonstone! Rachel thought excitedly. *No wonder Ellie's been sleeping well. She must have been having extra-sweet dreams!*

"I'm just going to take Ellie inside," said Mrs Palmer. "There's a chill in the air, all of a sudden."

"I hope that doesn't mean that some of Jack Frost's goblins are nearby," Rachel murmured to herself.

Leaving Mrs Palmer wrapping Ellie in a blanket, Rachel ran down the garden towards Kirsty and India, who were searching round the birdbath in the middle of the lawn.

"I've found the Moonstone!" Rachel whispered triumphantly. "It's hanging in the middle of the mobile on Ellie's pram."

"Wonderful!" India gasped.

"Well done, Rachel!" added Kirsty.

"Mrs Palmer's taking Ellie inside," said Rachel. "We can get the Moonstone as soon as she's gone."

The girls and India watched as Mrs Palmer carried Ellie into the house. Then Rachel and Kirsty immediately ran towards the pram, with India flying along beside them. But before they reached it, the door of the garden shed flew open with a crash, and two green goblins rushed out!

"The Moonstone is ours!" one of the goblins yelled. "And we'll never let the fairies have it back!"

"Never! Never!" shouted the other goblin.

As Kirsty, Rachel and India watched in horror, he leapt up onto the pram and grabbed at the string on which the

Moonstone was dangling.

"He's going to take the Moonstone!" Rachel gasped. "Stop him!"

As the girls rushed towards the pram, the other goblin panicked. Hurriedly, he began pushing the pram off the patio, away from the girls. But the pram was much bigger than the goblin, who was only knee-high, and he couldn't control it properly.

It bumped and bounced over the grass and onto the garden path. The goblin inside was caught off-balance.

With a screech of rage, he tumbled
over and got caught up in the
baby's blankets, before he
could grab the Moonstone.

Kirsty, Rachel and India
chased after the pram
as the goblin charged
down the garden path,
pushing it in front of
him. They could see
the Moonstone swinging
wildly on the mobile,
but they couldn't reach
it – the goblins were too far ahead.
The pram bounced and jolted its way
along, while the goblin inside was
struggling to free himself from the
tangle of blankets, and he shouted
crossly at his friend to stop.

Then, all of a sudden, one wheel hit
a large stone lying in the middle of the
path. The pram was going so fast that
it overturned. Both goblins let out shrill
cries of alarm as they flew through the
air. And then they both landed in a
heap, covered in Ellie's sheets and
blankets, underneath a large fir tree.

"India, can you stop the goblins from getting away?" Kirsty panted, as she and Rachel chased down the path towards the goblins.

"I have a little dream magic left which might send the goblins to sleep," India replied.

She zoomed ahead of the girls and hovered over the goblins, waving her wand. A few sparkles of fairy dust drifted down onto the goblins, who stopped struggling to free themselves and began yawning and rubbing their eyes instead.

"I'm so tired!" one of them sighed.

"And this blanket is really warm and cosy," the other one said sleepily. "I think I might have a little nap."

"Me too," the first goblin agreed. "Sing me a lullaby."

"No, you sing a lullaby!" the second goblin demanded.

"No, YOU!" yelled the first.

"They're waking themselves up with their silly argument!" Rachel exclaimed. "What are we going to do?"

"I think I have an idea!" Kirsty whispered, hurrying towards the goblins.

Rock-a-bye Goblins

Rachel and India watched as Kirsty began to tuck the goblins snugly into the blanket.

"Now, now, settle down," she said in a soft, sweet voice. "It's time for your nap."

The goblins stopped arguing and started yawning again.

"I am sleepy," the first goblin
murmured, snuggling down under the
pink blanket.

But the second goblin was trying hard
to keep his eyes open. "Wasn't there
something we were supposed to be
doing?" he asked.

Rachel hurried over to help Kirsty. "Go
to sleep now," she said in a soothing
voice. "You can worry about that later."

And Kirsty began to sing a lullaby to
the tune of *Rock-a-bye Baby:*
  "Rock-a-bye Goblins wrapped in a rug,
  Asleep in the garden, all nice and snug,
  When you wake up from your little nap,
  You will find India's got her stone back."
By the second line of
Kirsty's little song,
both goblins were
snoring soundly.

  "Well done,
Kirsty," Rachel said
with a grin. "But we
can't leave the goblins
here for Mrs Palmer to find!"

  "Leave that to me," India replied. She
waved her wand over a large branch
of the fir tree. Immediately, the branch
drooped lower, so that the leaves

completely covered the sleeping goblins.

"Perfect!" Kirsty declared. "The goblins are green like the leaves, so they'll be well hidden until they wake up."

India and Rachel laughed.

"Then they'll have to rush back to Jack Frost and tell him they've lost the Moonstone," India said. "They'll be in big trouble!"

Chuckling quietly, the girls picked up the pram and pushed it back to the patio. Then, as India watched in delight, Kirsty carefully took the magic Moonstone from the middle of the mobile. It flashed and gleamed in the sunlight.

"We mustn't spoil Ellie's mobile," India said. She waved her wand and a glittering, shiny bubble appeared in place of the Moonstone on the mobile.

As it caught the light, it sent rainbow-colours shining in all directions.

"And now," India went on, "the Moonstone is going straight back to Fairyland and the Queen's tiara, where it belongs!" She touched her wand to the jewel. Immediately a fountain of sparkling fairy dust shot up into the air and the Moonstone vanished.

"Thank you, girls," India said, giving Rachel and Kirsty a hug. "I must go home now, but I hope you'll be able to help the other Jewel Fairies find their magic stones too."

"We'll do our best!" Rachel promised.

"Goodbye, India!" Kirsty added, as their fairy friend flew away in a cloud of sparkles.

"I wonder where the other six jewels are hiding," Rachel murmured.

"And I wonder if we'll have to face many more goblins," Kirsty said with a frown.

Rachel shivered, remembering her nightmare. "I just hope I don't dream about them again tonight," she said.

Kirsty laughed. "Don't worry, Rachel," she told her friend. "India's got the Moonstone back now; she's sure to send you sweet dreams!"

RAINBOW magic

The Jewel Fairies

India has got her moonstone back.
Now Rachel and Kirsty
must help

Scarlett the Garnet Fairy

Win a Rainbow Magic
Sparkly T-Shirt and Goody Bag!

In every book in the Rainbow Magic Jewel Fairies
series (books 22-28) there is a hidden picture of a jewel with
a secret letter in it. Find all seven letters and
re-arrange them to make a special Fairyland word,
then send it to us. Each month we will put the entries into a
draw and select one winner to receive a
Rainbow Magic Sparkly T-shirt and Goody Bag!

Send your entry on a postcard to Rainbow Magic Jewel
Competition, Orchard Books, 96 Leonard Street,
London EC2A 4XD. Australian readers should
write to Hachette Children's Books, Level 17/207
Kent Street, Sydney, NSW 2000.
Don't forget to include your name and address.
Only one entry per child. Final draw: 30th September 2006.

Coming Soon...

Stella the Star Fairy

STELLA THE STAR FAIRY

1-84362-869-4

Stella the Star Fairy can't keep Christmas bright and shiny without her three magical tree decorations. Can Kirsty and Rachel help her get them back to the fairy tree by Christmas Eve, or will the season be ruined for everyone?

RAINBOW magic ®

by Daisy Meadows

The Jewel Fairies

Coming Soon: The Pet Fairies

All priced at £3.99. *Holly the Christmas Fairy, Summer the Holiday Fairy*
and *Stella the Star Fairy* are priced at £4.99.
Rainbow Magic books are available from all good bookshops, or can be ordered
direct from the publisher: Orchard Books, PO BOX 29, Douglas IM99 1BQ
Credit card orders please telephone 01624 836000
or fax 01624 837033 or visit our Internet site: www.wattspub.co.uk
or e-mail: bookshop@enterprise.net for details.

To order please quote title, author and ISBN and your full name and address.
Cheques and postal orders should be made payable to 'Bookpost plc.'
Postage and packing is FREE within the UK
(overseas customers should add £2.00 per book).
Prices and availability are subject to change.

Have you checked out the

Website at:
www.rainbowmagic.co.uk

There are games, activities and
fun things to do, as well as news
and information about Rainbow
Magic and all of the fairies.

Have you checked out the

Website at:

www.rainbowmagic.co.uk

There are games, activities and fun things to do, as well as news and information about Rainbow Magic and all of the fairies.

All priced at £3.99. *Holly the Christmas Fairy*, *Summer the Holiday Fairy*
and *Stella the Star Fairy* are priced at £4.99.
Rainbow Magic books are available from all good bookshops, or can be ordered
direct from the publisher: Orchard Books, PO BOX 29, Douglas IM99 1BQ
Credit card orders please telephone 01624 836000
or fax 01624 837033 or visit our Internet site: www.wattspub.co.uk
or e-mail: bookshop@enterprise.net for details.

To order please quote title, author and ISBN and your full name and address.
Cheques and postal orders should be made payable to 'Bookpost plc.'
Postage and packing is FREE within the UK
(overseas customers should add £2.00 per book).
Prices and availability are subject to change.

RAINBOW magic®

The Jewel Fairies

To Josephine Scarlet Whitehouse
– a little jewel, herself

Special thanks to
Sue Mongredien

ORCHARD BOOKS
96 Leonard Street, London EC2A 4XD
Hachette Children's Books
Level 17/207 Kent Street,
Sydney, NSW 2000
A Paperback Original
First published in Great Britain in 2005 as 1 84362 954 2
Rainbow Magic is a registered trademark of Working Partners Limited.
Series created by Working Partners Limited, London W6 0QT
Text © Working Partners Limited 2005
Illustrations © Georgie Ripper 2005
The right of Georgie Ripper to be identified as the illustrator
of this work has been asserted by her in accordance
with the Copyright, Designs and Patents Act, 1988.

Scarlett the Garnet Fairy

by Daisy Meadows

illustrated by Georgie Ripper

ORCHARD BOOKS

www.rainbowmagic.co.uk

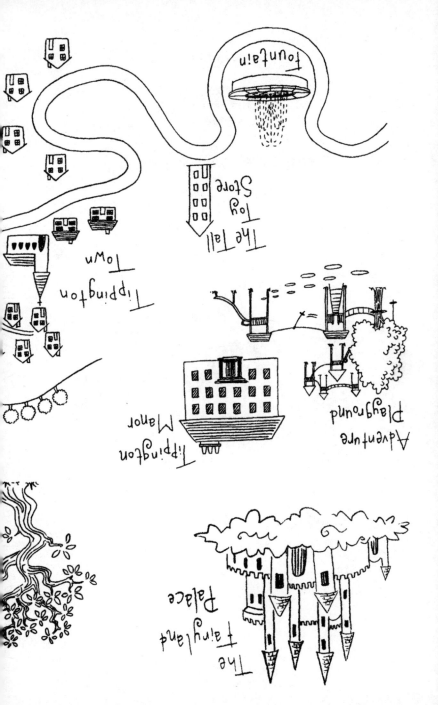

Chestnut
Tree

Buttercup
Farm

Scarecrow

Rachel's
House

Cherrywell Village

FANCY DRESS

Pegasus

Jack Frost's
Ice Castle

Twisty
Tree

By Frosty magic I cast away
These seven jewels with their fiery rays,
So their magic powers will not be felt
And my icy castle shall not melt.

The fairies may search high and low
To find the gems and take them home.
But I will send my goblin guards
To make the fairies' mission hard.

Contents

A Walk on the Farm

"Wakey, wakey!" Rachel Walker called, bouncing on the end of her friend Kirsty's bed. Kirsty Tate was staying with the Walker family for the October half-term holiday and Rachel didn't want to waste a single second.

Kirsty yawned and stretched. "I just had the most amazing dream," she said sleepily.

"Queen Titania asked us to help the
Jewel Fairies find seven stolen
gemstones from her magic tiara
and…" Her voice trailed away and
she opened her eyes wide. "It wasn't a
dream, was it?" she said, sitting bolt
upright. "We really did meet India the
Moonstone Fairy yesterday!"

Rachel nodded, smiling. "We
certainly did," she agreed.

Kirsty and Rachel shared a wonderful secret. They were friends with the fairies! They had had all sorts of fantastic adventures with them in the past – and now the fairies were in trouble.

Mean Jack Frost had stolen the seven magical jewels from the Fairy Queen's tiara. He had wanted to keep the jewels for himself, but their magic was so powerful that his ice castle had begun to melt. In a rage, Jack Frost had hurled the jewels away, and now they were lost.

King Oberon and Queen Titania had asked the girls to help return the jewels to Fairyland. Yesterday, Kirsty and Rachel had helped India the Moonstone Fairy find the magic Moonstone. But there were still six jewels left to find.

"I'm glad the Moonstone is safely back in Fairyland," Rachel said. "And I had a lovely dream last night, so we know for sure that India's dream magic is working properly again now."

The Fairy King and Queen had told the girls that the jewels from Queen Titania's tiara controlled some of the most important kinds of fairy magic. Every year, in a special ceremony, the fairies would replenish their magic by dipping their wands in the magical fountain that streamed from the tiara. But Jack Frost had stolen the jewels just before this year's ceremony could take place. And that meant that all the fairies were running low on much of their special fairy magic.

"We've just got to find the other
jewels before the fairies' magic is gone,"
Kirsty said, getting dressed quickly.
"Perhaps we'll discover another jewel
today!"

Rachel agreed eagerly and
together the girls
hurried downstairs
for breakfast.
Unfortunately,
it drizzled all
morning and there
was no sign of any
jewels or any fairies.

After lunch, though, the clouds cleared
away to reveal a blue sky and sunshine.

"Who wants to come with me
to Buttercup Farm?" Mrs Walker
asked, clearing away the lunch things.

"We need some vegetables and eggs for tea – and you two look like you need some fresh air."

"We do!" Rachel agreed, grinning at Kirsty. She held up crossed fingers while her mum wasn't looking. "We might come across a jewel," she added in a whisper.

A few minutes later, the girls and Mrs Walker set off down the lane towards the farm. Buttons, the Walkers' dog, trotted happily alongside them, sniffing at interesting smells in the hedgerow.

"He loves coming to the farm," Rachel told Kirsty, patting Buttons. "He's known the Johnsons' sheepdog, Cloud, since they were both pups, and the two of them go crazy whenever they see each other. Don't you, boy?"

"Woof!" barked Buttons, as if he was agreeing with her.

As the girls strolled along, something caught Kirsty's eye. "Look at those," she said, pointing to some red and white toadstools under a tree. "They're exactly like the Fairyland toadstool houses, aren't they?" Rachel nodded. "Oh, I do hope we meet another fairy today, Kirsty!" she said.

Kirsty crunched happily through the fallen leaves. "You know what Queen Titania always says," she whispered, as Mrs Walker bent down and let Buttons off his lead. "Don't go looking for magic…"

"It will find you!" Rachel finished.

Kirsty linked her arm through Rachel's. "It is hard not to look, though," she confessed. "I keep wondering where we're going to meet our next fairy – and who it's going to be!"

"Here we are," Mrs Walker said, as they turned off the lane into a long driveway. An old stone farmhouse stood at the end of the drive, with a pretty thatched roof and wood smoke curling from the chimney.

A smiling woman opened the front door. "Hello," she called warmly. "Come in, all of you. Oh, Buttons, too, Cloud will be pleased."

"This is my friend Kirsty. She's staying with us," Rachel said. "And Kirsty, this is Mrs Johnson."

"Hello," Kirsty said, returning Mrs Johnson's smile.

"Nice to meet you, Kirsty," Mrs Johnson said, leading the way into the sunny farmhouse kitchen. "I've just picked the last plums from my plum tree. Would anyone like one?"

"Yes, please," the girls chorused.

A volley of barking greeted them as they went in, and Cloud, a black and white sheepdog, danced around their legs. Buttons romped joyfully after him, barking just as noisily.

"Shall we take the dogs out for a walk?" Rachel offered quickly, as Buttons' tail almost knocked over a basket of eggs.

"Good idea," Mrs Johnson replied, giving the girls a handful of plums each. "Oh," she added, as they were about to head out of the door, "I should warn you that Mr Johnson is in rather a bad mood. His new green tractor has disappeared and he thinks one of the farm lads has taken it for a ride." She winked at the girls. "So if you see him and he's a bit grumpy, just ignore him, won't you?"

The girls nodded and followed Buttons and Cloud out of the door and into the meadows. Suddenly, Cloud trotted back over to the girls looking

very pleased with himself. He dropped something at their feet.

"What's this?" Kirsty asked, bending to pick it up. "Oh, look, Rachel," she said. "It's a tiny toy tractor." She giggled. "Do you think we should give it to Mr Johnson to make up for the one he's lost?"

Rachel grinned. "I don't think he'd appreciate it," she replied. "We'd better leave it here, in case somebody comes back for it."

Kirsty put the tractor down on a flat
bit of grass where it was easy to spot.
As she straightened up, she noticed
some odd-looking, shiny stones. "Are
those rocks over there?" she asked in a
puzzled voice.

Rachel turned and looked where her
friend was pointing. She saw several

large brown objects
under a chestnut tree
on one side of the
meadow. "That's
strange," she said,
frowning. "I've
never noticed them
before. Let's go and
have a closer look."

Kirsty and Rachel
ran across to the tree.

The brown objects Kirsty had spotted
were roughly the size and shape of
footballs, and they were
a glossy, chocolate
brown colour.
"Well, they're
not rocks,"
Kirsty said,
stroking one
of them. It felt cool
and smooth under her palm.
"They look more like…giant
chestnuts!"

Rachel patted one curiously.
"They do look like chestnuts," she
agreed. "But whoever heard of a
chestnut this size?"

Before Kirsty could reply, Buttons
bounded over, yapping excitedly.

Then he ran back to a patch of grass a few metres away, sniffed it eagerly and barked again.

Rachel went to see what he'd found. "Kirsty, quick!" she called, her eyes wide. "Come and look at these sheep!"

"Sheep?" echoed Kirsty, incredulously, running over to join Rachel. She couldn't see any sheep, yet as she got nearer to her friend she heard a tiny, but distinct, "Ba-a-a-a-a!"

Rachel pointed down at the grass and Kirsty's gaze followed her finger.

"Tiny sheep!" Kirsty gasped in surprise. "Oh, my goodness! Are they real?"

Down at their feet was a flock of the tiniest sheep Kirsty and Rachel had ever seen. Sheep, the size of mice! Chestnuts, the size of footballs! Whatever was going on?

Rachel's eyes were bright. "There is definitely magic in the air today," she breathed.

"There must be another magic jewel somewhere nearby," Kirsty added, feeling a thrill of excitement.

Hurriedly, the girls put the dogs on their leads and tied them to the fence, so that the tiny sheep would be safe.

Then Rachel clutched Kirsty's arm. "Kirsty!" she squeaked. "Look!"

Both girls stared. Floating down from the chestnut tree in front of them was a large golden leaf – and there, sitting on top of it as if she was riding a magic carpet, was a tiny beaming fairy.

Seeing Red

"Wheeeeee!" squealed the fairy
breathlessly. "Hello, girls!"

Kirsty and Rachel laughed in
delight as the golden leaf sailed down
to the ground. The fairy promptly
jumped off and twirled up into the
air, her wings beating so quickly
they were a blur of glittering colours.

She had curly dark brown hair, and she
wore a scarlet dress decorated with a
pretty flower where the hemline rose at
the front. She also wore little, glittery
red shoes which twinkled in the sunlight.

"It's Scarlett the Garnet Fairy," Rachel
declared, recognising her instantly.
"Hello, Scarlett."

"Of course!" Kirsty said,
clapping her hands
as she remembered
something King
Oberon had told
them. "The Garnet
controls growing and
shrinking magic, doesn't
it?" she exclaimed. "That's
why the chestnuts are so enormous…"

"And the sheep are so tiny," Rachel
added, with a smile.

"Exactly," Scarlett said. She waved
her wand hopefully, but only a few red
sparkles scattered from it. Kirsty watched
as they fizzled and spluttered out in the
grass. "And unfortunately, without it,
I don't have enough magic to turn
things back to their proper sizes,"

Scarlett explained sadly.
"We must find the
Garnet before
it changes
anything else."

She flew over to
perch on Kirsty's
shoulder. "India
told me that you had
a run-in with Jack Frost's
goblins yesterday," she said, shivering at
the thought. "Let's try and find the
Garnet before any goblins get here."

"We'll start right away," Rachel said
immediately, and Kirsty nodded.

"Great," Scarlett replied, with a smile.
"I'll try the vegetable patch over there."

"And we'll search this field," Kirsty
said. "Come on, Rachel."

32

The girls set off across the meadow, scanning the grass for any sign of the Garnet. They were just passing a haystack, when something very strange happened.

"My legs are tingling!" Kirsty gasped.

"We're shrinking!" Rachel cried, as she saw the ground rushing towards her.

The girls had often been fairy-sized before – but then they'd always had pretty wings to fly with too! But not this time – suddenly the haystack seemed like a mountain in front of them, and the grass was waist-high.

"The Garnet must be very close, if the magic is working on us now," Kirsty pointed out.

"Scarlett! Hey, Scarlett!" Rachel shouted, trying to attract the attention of the Garnet Fairy. But her voice had shrunk, too – and Scarlett didn't hear her tiny call.

"Rachel, look at the top of the haystack," Kirsty cried, pointing upwards. "It's glowing red!"

Rachel looked up at once, and sure enough, something at the top of the haystack did seem to be shining a deep red colour. "It must be the Garnet!" she declared. "Let's climb up and get it for Scarlett."

"Good idea," Kirsty agreed.

The two girls began to climb the haystack. It was very hard work because the hay was sharp and slippery and it was difficult to get a firm grip on the smooth stalks, but little by little the girls drew closer to the magic Garnet.

Just as Kirsty was about to reach the top, the stalk she was holding onto suddenly swayed and bent. Kirsty lunged for something else to grab, and clutched at another stalk, but it promptly snapped in two! "Help!" cried Kirsty, desperately trying to hang on. "I'm falling!"

A Scary Surprise

"Here!" Rachel yelled, leaning down to reach Kirsty. "Grab my hand!"

Kirsty clung onto her friend's outstretched fingers, her heart pounding as her feet scrabbled for a safe foothold. "Thanks," she said shakily, as her feet found a strong straw and Rachel helped pull her upwards.

The girls clambered gingerly up the
last few steps – and then Rachel gave a
triumphant cry. "We've found it!" she
cheered, for there in front of them lay
the glittering red Garnet. The sun shone
through it, casting a rich, rosy light
across the hay.

"Wow!" breathed Kirsty. It seemed
even more impressive
now the girls were
fairy-sized. The
jewel was no
bigger than a
hen's egg, but
right now that
was almost as
tall as Rachel
and Kirsty!

"Scarlett!" both
girls shouted. They
waved their arms around
at the top of the haystack, hoping the
fairy would see or hear them.

But Scarlett was still searching hard in
the vegetable patch, completely
unaware that her jewel had been found.

Then Kirsty had a good idea. "What if we turn the Garnet round so that its red light shines across to Scarlett?" she suggested. "That's sure to get her attention."

"Brilliant," Rachel agreed. "I bet it's heavy, though. I think we'll have to lift it together."

Kirsty took hold of one side of the jewel and Rachel held the other. Then, Kirsty counted, "One…two…three!" and together the girls heaved the gemstone around, so that its rosy light was shining directly at Scarlett.

The little fairy turned at once, and
when she saw the girls with the
Garnet her face lit up.
"Yippee!" she cried,
leaping into the air
and twirling for joy.
"Well done!"
Kirsty and
Rachel both
took a hand
off the Garnet
to wave at her.
As they did so,
the magic stone
slipped slightly and
its sparkling red light
danced further along the
vegetable patch, flickering over
a scarecrow that stood nearby.

And then, to the girls' great surprise, the scarecrow moved!

Rachel and Kirsty stared in amazement as the scarecrow jumped down from its wooden stand and started lumbering its way towards the haystack.

"What's happening?" Rachel asked. "Is it more fairy magic, do you think?"

"I don't know," Kirsty replied doubtfully. "I didn't think the Garnet could do that." She watched the scarecrow walking jerkily towards them, and suddenly felt nervous. "It's coming over here. What do you think it wants?"

Rachel narrowed her eyes and stared hard at the scarecrow. "Hang on a minute," she said. "Look at its green, pointy nose. That's not a scarecrow – it's a goblin!"

"Oh, no!" Kirsty cried, clutching Rachel in fright. "Look how enormous it is!"

"It's as big as a man," Rachel said anxiously, biting her lip. All of a sudden, she felt smaller than ever. How would she and Kirsty protect the Garnet when they were so tiny and the goblin was so huge? "Oh, do be quick, Scarlett! Come and get this Garnet!" she yelled frantically.

Scarlett was flying over as fast as she could, a determined look on her face. "I'm coming," she cried. "Hang on, girls!"

Kirsty gulped, still holding onto Rachel. "Look!" she said, pointing at the scarecrow.

For it had stopped walking and was now pulling off its long coat. And underneath the coat there wasn't just one goblin, there were two – one standing on the other's shoulders. The top goblin jumped down, and as Rachel and Kirsty watched in horror, both goblins started running as fast as they could towards the Garnet – and the girls.

Kidnapped!

"Let's get out of here," Kirsty cried
fearfully. As quickly as they could, she
and Rachel began to clamber back down
the haystack, carrying the Garnet
between them. The jewel felt strangely
warm as they held it.

"My fingers are tingling," Rachel called
out. "Do you think that means—?"

But Rachel's words were cut off,
because the Garnet's magic was working
again – and this time both girls were
growing. They clung tightly to the jewel
as their legs lengthened,
and their heads shot
up towards the sky.
Suddenly, the haystack,
which had seemed such
a mountain to climb,
was nothing more
than a regular
haystack – and it
couldn't hold the
weight of the two girls. 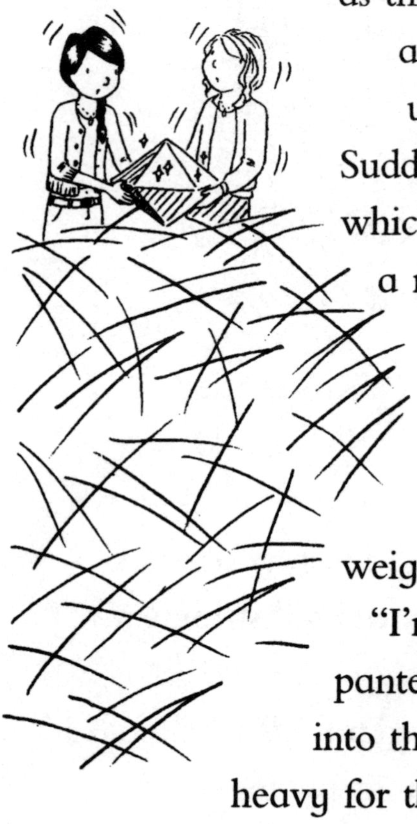
"I'm sinking," Rachel
panted, as her feet sunk
into the hay. "We're too
heavy for the haystack now."

Scarlett arrived at that moment, her face anxious. "I'll try and magic you out of there!" she cried, waving her wand quickly. But only one glittering red sparkle fell out and fizzled uselessly on the grass. "Uh-oh, here come the goblins!" she wailed, fluttering protectively in front of Kirsty and Rachel.

"Oh dear, oh dear," chortled the taller goblin who had been at the bottom of the scarecrow. He watched, sniggering, as the girls floundered around in the waist-deep hay.

The other, shorter goblin was close behind. "I think we'll have that Garnet, thank you," he declared, reaching out to snatch it from Rachel's hand.

"Oh, no, you don't!" Rachel cried, throwing the precious stone into the air before the goblin could grab it.

"Catch, Scarlett!"

Scarlett nimbly caught the Garnet just in time, but in the human world it was too big and heavy for her to fly with. She sunk rapidly downwards under the weight of the jewel, desperately flapping her wings as hard as she could.

Kirsty could see that Scarlett was trying to angle her wand so that it would touch the stone, and she realised that the little fairy was hoping to recharge her wand with growing and shrinking magic. But before she could do so, poor Scarlett lost her grip on the

wand and it tumbled down into the hay. Luckily, Kirsty pounced on the wand before either of the goblins could reach it, but then something terrible happened. The shorter goblin whipped off the scarecrow hat he still had on his head and held it out beneath the falling fairy.

"Help!" Scarlett cried, as she plunged helplessly into the dark hat.

"Gotcha!" cheered the goblin. "A Garnet and a fairy – that's a bonus!"

"Hey!" called Rachel, kicking out at the hay in an attempt to get free of it. "Bring Scarlett back, right now!"

"No chance!" both goblins laughed nastily – and away they ran.

As the two girls scrambled out of the haystack, the goblins pelted across the field with Scarlett and the Garnet still trapped inside the scarecrow hat. Kirsty and Rachel could hear them singing jubilantly:

"Twinkle, twinkle, Garnet stone,
You are never going home.
Jack Frost wants you hidden away.
Out of Fairyland you shall stay.
Sparkle, sparkle, on and on
The fairies' magic will soon be gone!"

"Come back!" shouted Kirsty angrily.
"Rachel, we've got to get that
scarecrow hat before it's too late!"

Dogs to the Rescue

As Rachel and Kirsty scrambled out of the hay, they looked wildly around for anything that would help them rescue Scarlett. Then Kirsty's gaze fell upon Cloud and Buttons, and she remembered that in the past the goblins had been scared of dogs. "Wait," she called, thinking fast.

"Maybe Buttons and Cloud can help
us!"

The dogs already seemed to have
had the same idea. They were both
straining at their leads and barking
at the goblins.

"Come on, boy," Rachel said, letting
Buttons off his lead.
"Let's go goblin
catching!"
"And you, Cloud,"
Kirsty said,
releasing him too.
"Go, dogs, go!"
Cloud and Buttons
did not need telling
twice. With a rousing
chorus of barks, they both
hurtled eagerly towards the goblins.

The goblin who was carrying the
scarecrow hat looked over his shoulder
and screeched with fear when
he saw the dogs. "Quick!"
he yelled to his friend.
"Get back up the
scarecrow stand!"

Both goblins
scrambled back up
the wooden stand
that had supported
them in their
scarecrow disguise,
and clung tightly
to its beams.

"Woof! Woof! Woof!"
Buttons and Cloud barked
happily, jumping up at the stand
and trying to lick the goblins' toes.

"Eek!" yelped the tall goblin, drawing his feet up. "Shoo, you horrible mutts!"

Kirsty and Rachel ran over. "This is all your fault," they heard the tall goblin hiss at his friend. "It was your idea to climb up here!"

"Well, if you'd run a bit quicker, we could have been out of here by now," the short one moaned back.

"Everything all right?" Kirsty asked sweetly, patting Cloud and Buttons who were still looking hopefully up at the goblins, and wanting to play.

"No!" snapped the tall goblin sulkily.

"Just call the dogs off!" the short goblin begged.

"No chance," Rachel replied cheerfully. "Unless…"

"What? What?" the goblins cried together.

"Unless you set Scarlett free," Kirsty finished.

The short goblin looked thoughtful and scratched his leathery, green head. "All right," he said at last, "the fairy can go – but the Garnet's staying right here, in my hat."

"OK," the girls agreed.

Rachel grabbed both dogs by their collars and held them back. "Now, let Scarlett go," she said.

The goblin cautiously opened the
hat just wide enough for Scarlett
to flutter out.

She zoomed through the
gap and flew to Kirsty's
shoulder. "Thank you,"
she said, as Kirsty
gave her her wand
back. "That
hat smelled awful!"

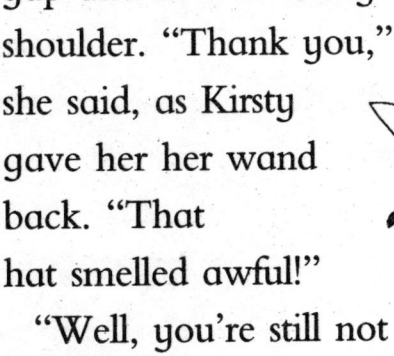

"Well, you're still not
getting your hands on our jewel," the
goblin said firmly, reaching into the hat
to pat the Garnet protectively, "so you
might as well— Hey!" he suddenly
yelped in surprise. "What's happening?"

Kirsty, Rachel and Scarlett all stared
at the goblin. And then all three of
them began to chuckle.

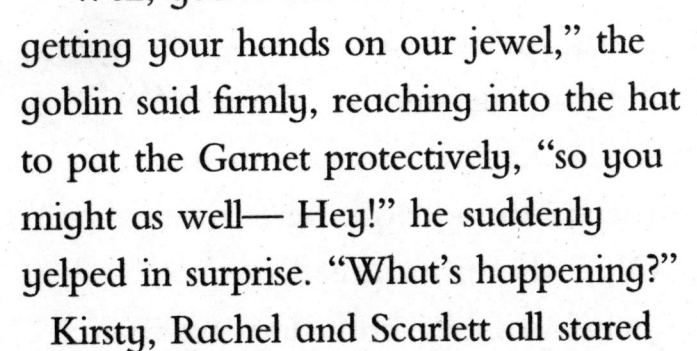

"It's the Garnet!" Scarlett laughed.
"It's making him shrink!"

Sure enough, the short
goblin was growing
even shorter before
their eyes. "Help!
Make it stop!" he
squeaked in a tiny voice.

His friend was guffawing loudly — but
not for long. Now that there was one
big goblin and one tiny goblin on the
wooden stand, the whole thing was
starting to overbalance.

"Whoa!" the big goblin cried as he felt
himself falling. "Help!"

Goblins on the Run

Splat!

The girls backed out of the way just as the large goblin landed heavily on the ground. "Oof!" he panted. "Stupid Garnet!"

"Woof!" barked the dogs, running over and licking the goblin playfully. "Woof! Woof!"

Rachel and Kirsty couldn't help
smiling as the goblin rolled around,
helpless with laughter. "It tickles!" he
roared. "Ooh, it tickles!"

Then Kirsty remembered the Garnet.
She rushed over to the scarecrow pole
where the tiny goblin was still hanging
on – and plucked the hat easily from
his grasp.

"Hurrah!" cheered Scarlett as she saw the magic Garnet gleaming in Kirsty's hand. "Well done, Kirsty!"

"We did it!" Rachel beamed. "That's another jewel found."

The girls and Scarlett headed back towards the farmhouse, calling the dogs to follow them once they were a safe distance from the goblins.

Scarlett carefully touched her wand to the magic Garnet and waved it in the air. A stream of glittering, red fairy dust flooded out across the fields and a smile lit Scarlett's face. "That's more like it," she said thankfully.

Baa! Baa! The sheep were suddenly back to their normal size. Cloud and Buttons stared at them in confusion, wondering where they had come from.

Cloud sniffed at a stray red sparkle and jumped as it fizzed into thin air under his nose.

Kirsty turned to look at the chestnut tree. The giant chestnuts had disappeared – they had shrunk to their normal size again – and what was this, standing in the middle of the field?

"Mr Johnson's tractor!" Rachel laughed. "The Garnet must have shrunk that, too – remember we thought it was a toy?"

Kirsty grinned as the last few, bright twinkles of fairy magic disappeared from the tractor's wheels. "Mr Johnson will be in a good mood again, now," she said happily.

"And so will King Oberon and Queen Titania when I magic this Garnet back to Fairyland," Scarlett added.

The tiny goblin had been turned back to his usual size too. The girls and Scarlett watched as he jumped down from the wooden stand and stomped away with his goblin friend. Although the girls couldn't hear what they were saying, it was clear that they were arguing again.

Scarlett chuckled. "And that's
the last we'll see of them,"
she said, sounding
satisfied. She touched
her wand to the
Garnet once more and
it vanished in a fountain
of glittering red fairy dust.

"And the Garnet's safely back in
Fairyland," Rachel commented with
a sigh of relief, as the air where
the Garnet had been shimmered for a
second and then returned to normal.

"And I should be going back too,"
Scarlett added, hugging the girls
goodbye. "Thank you for all your help,
Kirsty and Rachel. And good luck
finding the other magic jewels!"

The girls waved as the tiny fairy

zoomed away to Fairyland.

"Phew," Rachel said, as they neared
the farmhouse. "That was close. I thought
the goblins were going to get away with
the Garnet *and* Scarlett then."

Kirsty ruffled Cloud's shaggy coat
affectionately. "Well, thanks
to these two dogs, both
Scarlett and the Garnet
are safe and sound," she
declared with a smile.

Rachel grinned at Kirsty.
"Come on," she said, breaking
into a run. "I'm starving. I wonder if Mrs
Johnson has got any of those plums left."

"I hope so," Kirsty said, running
towards the house. "Race you there!"

RAINBOW magic ®

The Jewel Fairies

India and Scarlett have got their
jewels back. Now Rachel
and Kirsty must help

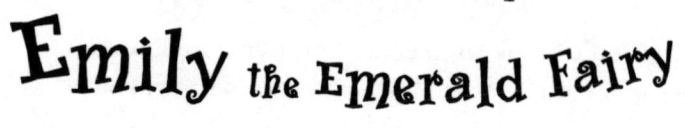

Emily the Emerald Fairy

Win a Rainbow Magic
Sparkly T-Shirt and Goody Bag!

In every book in the Rainbow Magic Jewel Fairies
series (books 22-28) there is a hidden picture of a jewel with
a secret letter in it. Find all seven letters and
re-arrange them to make a special Fairyland word,
then send it to us. Each month we will put the entries into a
draw and select one winner to receive a
Rainbow Magic Sparkly T-shirt and Goody Bag!

Send your entry on a postcard to Rainbow Magic Jewel
Competition, Orchard Books, 96 Leonard Street,
London EC2A 4XD. Australian readers should
write to Hachette Children's Books, Level 17/207
Kent Street, Sydney, NSW 2000.
Don't forget to include your name and address.
Only one entry per child. Final draw: 30th September 2006.

Coming Soon...
Stella the Star Fairy

STELLA THE STAR FAIRY

1-84362-869-4

Stella the Star Fairy can't keep Christmas
bright and shiny without her three magical
tree decorations. Can Kirsty and Rachel
help her get them back to the fairy tree
by Christmas Eve, or will the season
be ruined for everyone?

by Daisy Meadows